CHILDREN'S THRIFT CLASSICS

The Three Musketeers

ALEXANDRE DUMAS *père*

English Adaptation by Alan Weissman
Illustrated by John Green

DOVER PUBLICATIONS, INC.
New York

DOVER CHILDREN'S THRIFT CLASSICS
EDITOR OF THIS VOLUME: THOMAS CROFTS

Note

ALEXANDRE DUMAS *père* (so called because his son—Alexandre Dumas *fils*—was also a famous author) published *The Three Musketeers* in 1844.

Specializing in plays and novels with historical settings (including a play about Napoleon), Dumas *père* was known for his thrilling, rambunctious and passionate tales. *The Three Musketeers*, one of his best, is set in seventeenth-century France. The historical background, such as the siege of La Rochelle, is basically accurate, but the chief action, completely fictitious, is concerned with a heroic group of Musketeers (members of the King's private army) and a young gentleman swashbuckler named D'Artagnan.

Published in Canada by General Publishing Company, Ltd., 30 Lesmill Road, Don Mills, Toronto, Ontario.
Published in the United Kingdom by Constable and Company, Ltd., 3 The Lanchesters, 162–164 Fulham Palace Road, London W6 9ER.

Bibliographical Note

This Dover edition, first published in 1994, is a new English adaptation of *Les Trois Mousquetaires* (1844). The illustrations and introductory Note have been specially prepared for the present edition.

Library of Congress Cataloging-in-Publication Data

Weissman, Alan, 1947–
　The three musketeers / Alexandre Dumas ; English adaptation by Alan Weissman ; illustrated by John Green.
　　　p.　　cm. — (Dover children's thrift classics)
　In seventeenth-century France, young D'Artagnan initially quarrels with, then befriends, three musketeers and joins them in trying to outwit the enemies of the king and queen.
　ISBN 0-486-28326-7
　1. France—History—Louis XIII, 1610–1643—Juvenile fiction. [1. France—History—Louis XIII, 1610–1643—Fiction. 2. Adventure and adventurers—Fiction.] I. Dumas, Alexandre, 1802–1870. Trois mousquetaires. English. II. Green, John, 1948– ill. III. Title. IV. Title: 3 musketeers. V. Series.
PZ7.W448165Th 1994
[Fic]—dc20　　　　　　　　　　　　　　　　　　　　　　94-34998
　　　　　　　　　　　　　　　　　　　　　　　　　　　　　CIP
　　　　　　　　　　　　　　　　　　　　　　　　　　　　　AC

Manufactured in the United States of America
Dover Publications, Inc., 31 East 2nd Street, Mineola, N.Y. 11501

Contents

List of Illustrations

1

D'Artagnan Meets the Musketeers

L ONG AGO in France, on a bright spring morning—in April of 1626, to be exact—a young man from the country, of noble but somewhat awkward bearing, walked firmly down a lonely road outside Paris with the near-certain belief that within the hour he would be dead.

This eighteen-year-old gentleman, whose name was D'Artagnan, was newly arrived from Gascony, from which distant province he had come, as proud as he was poor, to pledge his service to the King, the Queen and the Cardinal. Yet he had not been in Paris for more than a few hours before he had somehow committed himself to fighting no fewer than three duels!

Now, this Cardinal, who was also a duke—the Duc de Richelieu—was almost as powerful as the King—some said even more powerful. He was always creating trouble, it seemed, even within the royal household. He had recently managed to raise suspicions in the King's mind against the Queen herself, accusing her of an unlawful relationship with the English Duke of

Buckingham. Alas, there was some truth to this charge. Both the Queen and the Cardinal had powerful networks of spies who helped them in their bitter rivalry.

The entire nation of France was the scene of great troubles then, there being violent hatred between the Catholics, led by Cardinal Richelieu, and a sect of French Protestants called the Huguenots, whose main stronghold was the coastal city of La Rochelle.

As D'Artagnan had plunged into this atmosphere of conflict, he was forced to take sides. Though as yet unable to join the elite band of the King's Musketeers, he had been allowed to join the lesser force of the King's Guards (who, with the Musketeers, were rivals of the Cardinal's Guards). He also had dared hope that perhaps he would become the valiant knight of some beautiful damsel in distress.

D'Artagnan had other problems. On his way to Paris, in the town of Meung, he had been mocked by a mysterious, evil-looking blackguard, evidently of high rank, with an ugly scar on his temple, who had set his servants to thrash him. Then, before D'Artagnan could deal with him properly, in gentlemanly sword-to-sword combat, the man, after exchanging mysterious words with an even more mysterious lady in a coach, had sped off on his horse like a coward.

Now came the greatest trouble of all. The three men with whom D'Artagnan was about to fight duels were all Musketeers! It had all come about because of some silly words of anger exchanged between D'Artagnan and the Musketeers in the mansion of Monsieur de Tréville, their leader.

By now, walking along under the hot sun, his sword flapping against his leg at his left hand, D'Artagnan had approached a grim windowless building surrounded by bare fields, part of a convent on the outskirts of Paris. Just then a clock in a nearby tower struck twelve and D'Artagnan, aware that he was about to meet his fate and very likely leave this earth, saw before him the noble figure of Athos, one of the Musketeers.

Athos, though in pain, the result of a wound he had received in another duel, stepped forward to meet his adversary. D'Artagnan, on his part, took off his hat and bowed deeply.

"Monsieur," said Athos, "I have engaged two of my friends as seconds; I do not know why they are late, as it is not their habit."

"I have no seconds, Monsieur," replied D'Artagnan, "as I have just arrived in Paris. But I see you are suffering terribly. I have a balsam for wounds, which I freely offer you. Within three days you will be cured, and then—well, sir, it would then still do me great honor to be your man."

"I am afraid that in three days word of our plans would be certain to leak out and our combat would be prevented. But," said Athos, "your words are those of a true gentleman. There is one of my seconds, I believe."

Walking down the road the gigantic Porthos appeared.

"What!" cried D'Artagnan. "Is your first witness M. Porthos?"

"Does that disturb you?"

"Not at all—and is the second M. Aramis?" Aramis was just then coming up behind Porthos.

"Of course. Are you not aware that we are never seen one without the others, and that we are called, among the Musketeers and the guards, at court and in the city, Athos, Porthos and Aramis—or the Three Inseparables? But then, you would not know that since you are from—"

"Tarbes," said D'Artagnan.

"Porthos, this is the gentleman I am going to fight," said Athos, gesturing toward D'Artagnan and greeting his friend at the same time.

"Ah! What does this mean? It is with him that I also am going to fight!" said Porthos.

"But not before one o'clock," said D'Artagnan.

"And I also am going to fight this gentleman," said Aramis as he walked up.

"But not before two o'clock," said D'Artagnan.

"But what are you going to fight about, Athos?" asked Aramis.

"Faith! I don't well know. He hurt my shoulder. And you, Porthos?"

"We are going to fight because—we are going to fight!"

"We had a little discussion about dress," explained D'Artagnan tactfully.

"And you, Aramis?"

"Oh, ours is a theological quarrel."

"Yes, there is a passage in St. Augustine upon which we could not agree," said D'Artagnan.

At this sign of courteous evasion Athos smiled slightly, thinking, "Decidedly this is a clever fellow."

"And now, gentlemen," announced D'Artagnan, "should M. Athos succeed in dispatching me, I offer my apologies that I will be unable to fight as agreed. But for now—on guard!" With the most gallant air imaginable, D'Artagnan drew his sword.

"As you please, Monsieur," replied Athos, likewise drawing his weapon.

Thus the two stood, with swords crossed, when, from the other side of the nearby convent, a troop of five of the Cardinal's Guards marched into sight.

"The Cardinal's Guards!" cried Aramis and Porthos. "Sheathe your swords, gentlemen, sheathe your swords!"

But it was too late. The Guards' commander, a M. Jussac, advanced toward D'Artagnan and the Musketeers, followed by his men.

"So! Despite the Cardinal's edicts against dueling, I see you are fighting here! Sheathe your swords, if you please, and follow us. We will charge upon you if you disobey."

"There are five of them," said Athos quietly, as if to himself, "and we are but three. We shall be beaten and must die on the spot, for, on my part, I declare I will never again appear before our captain as a conquered man."

"Monsieur," said D'Artagnan, "allow me to correct your words, if you please! You said you were but three, but it appears to me we are four."

"But you are not one of us," said Porthos.

"That is true," replied D'Artagnan, "I have not the uniform but I have the heart of a Musketeer. I am with you. Try me, gentlemen, and I swear to you, by the honor of the name D'Artagnan, that I will not abandon you whether we prevail or are conquered."

"You are a brave fellow," said Athos.

"Well—have you decided?" asked Jussac.

"Yes," replied Athos. "We are to have the honor of charging you! Athos, Porthos, Aramis and D'Artagnan, forward!"

At this the nine combatants joined in a furious battle. While the Musketeers were fighting certain of the Cardinal's men, it fell to D'Artagnan to fight Jussac himself!

The heart of the young Gascon beat wildly—not from fear, which emotion he scarcely knew, but from the thought that here at last was the opportunity to prove his worth by fighting on the side of the King's Musketeers.

Jussac was a fine swordsman who had had much practice. Nevertheless, with far less experience, D'Artagnan combined the hot blood of youth with both sound theory and extreme agility. When, angered that his skill should be so thwarted by a mere youth, Jussac thrust out in hot haste, lowering his guard, D'Artagnan glided like a serpent beneath his weapon and passed his sword through his body. Jussac fell like a stone. He was seriously wounded, though still breathing.

The rest passed quickly. The Musketeers and D'Artagnan soon overcame the three Guardsmen who were still on their feet, disarming them and forcing a surrender. The wounded were carried under the porch of the convent, and the convent bell was rung.

As the victors returned to Paris, D'Artagnan was intoxicated with joy. The four walked down the street arm in arm.

"If I am not yet a Musketeer," said D'Artagnan to his new friends as he passed through the gateway of M. de Tréville's mansion, "at least I have entered upon my apprenticeship, haven't I?"

After this trial, D'Artagnan became a part of the circle of the three Musketeers, who grew much attached to their young comrade. The friendship that united these four men and the need they felt of seeing one another three or four times a day, whether for dueling, business or pleasure, caused them to be continually running after one another like shadows. Now they were "the Four Inseparables"!

2

An Errand for the Queen

A T THIS TIME, with the financial help of his friends, D'Artagnan rented lodgings from a wealthy merchant, one M. Bonacieux, and secured the services of a manservant named Planchet. In D'Artagnan's lodgings, especially when his duties perforce separated him from the Musketeers, they would all meet in the evenings. By candlelight and over wine, all would recount their adventures of the day, or, occasionally, of days gone by. When it came to the past, however, D'Artagnan noticed frequent gaps, especially in the discourse of Athos. Aramis often discussed his ambitions to leave the military life altogether and commence a career in the church. But, apart from this, in his case it was mainly the present he avoided discussing, especially the mysterious letters his manservant Bazin frequently brought him, the contents of which could instantly transform his face to an image of joy or of gloom. To his annoyance, Athos and Porthos sometimes joked about his having a secret mistress among the high nobility.

Porthos was the least secretive about his life, often boastful of the attention paid him by a woman he referred to as his "duchess." As Athos and Aramis had reason to believe, however—and failed not to chide him about—this "duchess" was a woman some years older, not very good-looking, and the wife of a minor government official. Besides returning Porthos's cavalier attitude with admiration, this woman provided him with something perhaps even more important to him: money, with which he would feed his vanity by attiring himself in splendor.

Athos's past was the most mysterious, although sometimes when he had taken too much wine—which was often enough—he would begin to tell some bizarre story, seemingly unconnected with anything else in his life, but which would suggest that something extremely unfortunate had happened to him years earlier.

And so the days passed. Despite the turmoil and all the half-secret dueling going on at this time, however, the ordinary life of a soldier when not on the battlefield could grow dreary, and D'Artagnan began to pine for excitement. It was not long before he was satisfied.

One evening, before the customary arrival of his friends, he heard a clatter and commotion in the rooms downstairs, the residence of the merchant M. Bonacieux and his young wife. Now, as D'Artagnan was aware, the merchant had gone away for a few days, leaving his wife alone under the protection of a few old servants.

"Help! Help!" came a cry from below. At this, D'Artagnan strapped on his sword and leaped down the stairs into the street where two men were attempting to carry off the merchant's wife. D'Artagnan made quick work of her two assailants, only one of whom was armed anyway, and sent them running, leaving the gasping, terrified Mme. Bonacieux in D'Artagnan's arms.

"Quick, Monsieur, take me away from here, I beg you. These men were trying to kidnap me."

D'Artagnan helped her up the stairs to his own apartment, where he sat her in a chair.

"Planchet! Some water for the young lady, if you please!" he cried. This necessary item having been brought, D'Artagnan signaled for his man to withdraw discreetly.

When the beautiful young lady had recovered some of her calm, she began to show some embarrassment. She only half looked D'Artagnan in the eye, saying,

"Monsieur, please forgive my imposition on your kindness, but I must impose upon it once more by inquiring if you know of any place I can stay to be safe."

"It seems, Madame, that you are involved in matters that grow too large for you to handle, is it not true?" D'Artagnan ventured somewhat daringly.

She was silent. D'Artagnan knew from gossip at M. de Tréville's that the Queen herself, who

D'Artagnan made quick work of her two assailants.

had her own circle of spies and informers, made frequent use of Mme. Bonacieux (who was a high-ranking personal servant of the Queen's) in her intrigues.

"Of course, I know you must be bound to secrecy," said D'Artagnan more gallantly, "but if you confide in me, I swear upon my honor as a gentleman and a loyal member of the King's Guards that your secret shall not pass my lips to any but a chosen few who can be trusted. I ask this only because I have become acquainted with those who might be in a position to assist you if only they knew the nature of your difficulty."

Now, D'Artagnan, if the truth were told, did not make this offer out of entirely disinterested motives. From the first he had been attracted to his beguiling young neighbor. He had even felt what might be termed love for this ravishing young woman. Though the morals of the period were somewhat loose, this feeling was sustained in him by a degree of genuine idealism. He justified to himself the idea that he might be her rescuer, even her lover, by the thought that her marriage to M. Bonacieux, a man twice her age, had been arranged by her family out of convenience only; it was evident that little love passed between the woman and her staid, stingy merchant of a husband. So here was a situation that afforded D'Artagnan the excitement that he had been craving, the opportunity to save the royalty of

France—and even the opportunity to be the knight of a lady in distress.

She hesitated, then said, in a soft, sweet voice, "You appear to be a brave young man who can be trusted . . . ."

Fired up by these words, D'Artagnan grew animated.

"By my honor, by the faith of a gentleman, I will do all that I can to serve the King and be agreeable to the Queen!"

"Well . . . I know of no one else I can trust. And . . . there is one . . . in a very high place who is in grave danger. If you could find the time for a mission of great importance, you will be well rewarded, so long as that is in my power. I dare not show myself near the Louvre now." (The Louvre was in those days still the palace of the French royal family.) "But—can I trust you with a password so you may gain admittance by a door I will tell you of?"

"I swear to you I will forget that password as soon as it has served its purpose!"

Mme. Bonacieux then gave D'Artagnan involved instructions for obtaining a letter from one of the Queen's servants. With this letter would be provided further instructions for its delivery. Here was a mission worthy of the greatest trust and courage!

"Now, Madame," said D'Artagnan, moving closer, sorely tempted to forget his restraint and plant a kiss on her youthful lips, "we must meanwhile decide where you might stay."

"Well, Monsieur," said she, much relieved by the hope of accomplishing a mission that would serve the Queen, yet also a bit frightened at the unanticipated sudden physical proximity of a man who was almost a stranger, "perhaps I may safely remain in my house one more night. Tomorrow my husband returns."

Suddenly she rose and walked quickly toward the stairway.

Feeling that it was just as well that he was thus able to avoid further temptation, D'Artagnan said,

"Very well. But should you require assistance, do not hesitate to call on me. Or if I am away on this most sacred mission, my servant Planchet will see to your safety."

Mme. Bonacieux turned once, nodded in gratitude, and disappeared down the stairs.

For half an hour, D'Artagnan sat, pondering the situation. Then, although it was already quite late, he seized his hat and cloak, and stole off toward the Louvre.

About midnight, with a low fire flickering in the fireplace, Planchet was dozing in a chair when the door burst open and in strode D'Artagnan, a satisfied look on his face.

"Planchet, my man! Up! There will be no sleeping until late tonight—tomorrow I ask for emergency leave—which I have no doubt M. de Tréville will assist me in obtaining—and by nightfall we will be off on a mission of great impor-

tance!—Oh, one other thing: has there been any
further disturbance downstairs?"

"No, Monsieur, it has been very quiet."

"Very good! Now let us have some nourishment. And then you must pack necessaries for a
week and see about our horses in the morning."

"Certainly, Monsieur."

The night passed without further incident.

The following day D'Artagnan spent in scurry-
ing about Paris, first to M. de Tréville, then to M.
d'Essart, the commander of the King's Guards,
and to the three Musketeers as well. M. de
Tréville, assured of the urgency of this mission
and its value to the Queen, inquired no further
and granted the Musketeers leave as well as his
intercession with M. d'Essart on D'Artagnan's
behalf.

The three Musketeers of course pledged their
full support. They all gathered in the evening at
their usual meeting place—D'Artagnan's lodgings—but their usual gaiety was tempered by a
sense of the importance of the mission on which
they were about to embark.

"Now," said Porthos, "let us lay down the plan
of campaign. Where do we go first?" There was
some disagreement and bickering, but soon they
worked out a scheme, suggested by Athos.
D'Artagnan carried a precious letter (no doubt
from the Queen herself!) to be delivered in
England to the Duke of Buckingham, but it was
decided that, in case D'Artagnan were to be

killed or wounded, only one Musketeer was necessary to take the letter and deliver it.

Some further details were determined, and then, "Well," said D'Artagnan, "I decide that we should adopt Athos's plan, and that we should set off before sunrise. And remember our motto: All for one and one for all!"

"Agreed!" shouted the three Musketeers in chorus.

3

D'Artagnan in England

A T TWO O'CLOCK in the morning, our four adventurers and their servants left Paris by the Barrière St. Denis. Not many would have attempted to interfere with their passage, as the appearance of the caravan was formidable.

They stopped for breakfast in Chantilly. So far, so good. Yet, they began to feel that they were being watched with suspicion. But they rode on without incident. An inn in Beauvais provided shelter that night. Again, nothing out of the ordinary occurred, except that on their departure the following morning, once more it seemed that the innkeeper was watching them too closely. When Athos sharply returned the stare, the man abruptly turned away.

On they went. In the early afternoon they had to go through a narrow pass between two embankments where some workers were filling in potholes in the unpaved road. Incredibly, the workers seemed scarcely to acknowledge the presence of the travelers. The horses, slipping in the mud, had a difficult time of it. Aramis, his patience exhausted, let loose a few choice words at the workmen. He received only an insolent remark in return.

"Whoa! Stop!" cried Aramis. "I am going to teach this fellow some manners!" At this, the entire party stopped and dismounted to confront the workmen. Suddenly from over the embankment several more men appeared, armed with muskets! Athos leaned over to D'Artagnan and quietly said in his ear, "I knew there was something odd about these workmen. This is an ambush. When the gunfire begins, you escape with Planchet and we will carry on as best we can."

D'Artagnan needed to hear no more. A volley of shots was already being exchanged between the false workers and the Musketeers' servants. D'Artagnan motioned to Planchet and they leaped on their horses and galloped off, managing to skirt the mud-filled holes. As they escaped with the precious letter, D'Artagnan had the utmost confidence that his companions would overcome their assailants. It was only a matter of time—time that D'Artagnan could not now afford to lose.

D'Artagnan and Planchet galloped on through woods and meadows. Late in the afternoon they came abreast of another who like D'Artagnan was obviously a gentleman. With his own servant he was galloping in a rush, apparently also toward the harbor at Calais. As it happened,

D'Artagnan and this stranger both stopped at the same inn on the margin of a wood outside the town. After having briefly refreshed themselves, they and their servants both left their horses in the care of the innkeeper, and soon they found themselves walking at a brisk pace through the wood toward the harbor.

"Monsieur," said the strange gentleman, "I see you are in a hurry. If I may be so bold as to inquire, is it your intention to sail for England?"

"It is," replied D'Artagnan, without saying more.

"Then I might save you the trouble. All ports have been placed under restriction. Unless you have express written permission from the King or Cardinal, it is impossible to get on board for any money."

At this interesting bit of news, D'Artagnan began to think.

"Monsieur!" said he, "urgent personal business makes it essential that I be in London by tomorrow morning. It would appear, from what you say, that you possess the necessary letter of permission. How much do you ask for it?"

The man stopped and faced D'Artagnan, at which the entire party halted. By now they were in a little wood outside of the town.

"I am very sorry, Monsieur," said the man, "but that is impossible. I have traveled sixty leagues in forty-four hours, and I must be in London by midday. Business of the King, you know!"

"I am sorry too, Monsieur. I have traveled the

same distance in forty hours and I must be in London by ten o'clock—on even more urgent business."

"That is indeed your business, Monsieur, certainly, but—"

D'Artagnan, desperate and convinced of the priority of his mission, abruptly drew his sword and motioned to Planchet.

"I am sorry, but I must have that letter. Hand it over instantly!"

"This is outrageous!" cried the stranger. "Lubin! My pistols!"

"Quick, Planchet, you take care of the lackey; I will manage the master!" Planchet, young, strong and vigorous, sprang upon the servant, got him in a stranglehold and wrenched his pistol free. Meanwhile D'Artagnan and the strange gentleman were lunging at each other with drawn swords. The stranger was young and agile but no match for D'Artagnan. After receiving a slight wound, D'Artagnan thrust his sword home and the man fell—not dead, but seriously wounded.

D'Artagnan helped Planchet subdue the servant, whom they gagged and tied to a tree. They propped his master next to him, D'Artagnan searched for and found the letter of permission, and in twenty minutes they had shown it to the governor of the port and were on board the vessel.

As the ship began to sail out of Calais harbor, D'Artagnan leaned on the rail and contemplated his situation. It was a very risky one indeed. Here he had stabbed and nearly killed a man, a high-ranking nobleman no less, for it turned out that this was one Comte de Wardes. Now D'Artagnan had to compound the felony by impersonating the man to gain admittance on board the ship. This was a very serious matter. But so was the well-being of the Queen!

Soon it was proved that his desperate haste and extreme actions had been justified. For they had been swaying over the briny waves for only a few minutes or so when D'Artagnan saw a flash and heard a detonation. That cannon shot meant that the port had now been entirely closed by the Cardinal's orders!

Night fell. The winds were poor and for some time D'Artagnan thought he would never make it to Dover. About ten o'clock, however, the boat docked. Then came the next problem: how to get to London. This was not easy for one who, like D'Artagnan, knew little English. Finally, a pair of post horses took them to London. Then, with difficulty, they discovered that the Duke of Buckingham was at Windsor with the King of England. At last D'Artagnan was admitted to the august presence of the French Cardinal's counterpart— the most powerful man in England, next to the King himself. D'Artagnan was awed by the splendor of the room into which he was admitted: high-ceilinged, hung with artistic treasures, worthy of a prince of the realm.

D'Artagnan bowed upon entering to face the Duke, still a young man, handsome, splendidly attired, truly worthy of the connection with the Queen of France. This connection was doubtless a reality, no matter the cost in international tension, even war, that such a simple personal alliance brought in its train. Fortunately for D'Artagnan, the Duke spoke fluent French.

D'Artagnan, bidden to sit before the Duke, knew immediately that he was in the presence of greatness. Firm as he was in his own purpose, assured as he was of his own courage and loyalty, he could not but be impressed by one who obviously possessed more nobility of heart and more power—combined with more reckless-ness—than almost any courtier in Europe. The King of England's favorite and one of the wealthi-est and handsomest men in the world, George Villiers, Duke of Buckingham, set the world in disarray at his fancy, and then calmed it accord-ing to his whimsy. Whatever his object, he stopped at no means to achieve it. Thus he had succeeded in obtaining the affection of the equally proud and noble Anne of Austria, Queen of France, flouting all the dangers of such a position—a position that was at this very moment bringing D'Artagnan before him. Who could pre-dict the consequences of this meeting?

D'Artagnan looked up and, even to his surprise, saw a magnificent portrait of the Queen of France herself—whom he just barely recognized, having seen her on only one occasion, and then imperfectly.

"So!" the Duke interrupted D'Artagnan's thoughts. "Where is this letter of utmost importance you have brought me, no doubt at the risk of your life?"

D'Artagnan glanced around them and saw that the servants had retired. "Yes. The letter," he murmured, and he reached into a hidden pocket, withdrawing a creased envelope.

"Good Heavens!" exclaimed the Duke. "This *is* serious!"

D'Artagnan, puzzled by this utterance, looked down and saw that the envelope was stained with blood and was partly cut through.

"Oh yes," said he, "there was a little problem at Calais. But," he said as he handed it over, "you observe that the seal remains unbroken."

The Duke, uncharacteristically betraying nervous agitation, quickly tore open the envelope and scrutinized its contents. After sitting in thought for a few minutes, his face growing redder, he carefully locked away the letter in a drawer. Suddenly he jumped up.

"You will excuse me for a moment."

The Duke left the room briefly. When he returned, he sat down again. He paused a moment, looked D'Artagnan in the eye, and spoke:

"Sir. You have already done enough to earn my eternal gratitude. If I may impose upon your

kindness further by requesting that you remain in
England two more days . . . ."

The Duke spoke these words courteously but
with an undertone of one more accustomed to
giving orders than requesting favors. Nevertheless D'Artagnan replied, "I think I have already
made it perfectly clear that I will do anything to
aid the Queen. I am at your service!"

"Well spoken!" The Duke paused and thought-
fully fingered his elegant mustache. "Given the
strange circumstances that bring us together and,
more important, your unquestioned loyalty to
your Queen, I think I may confide in you. Besides,
you may be able to do your Queen a further
service."

"I am listening."

"It has become clear," the Duke went on, "that
Anne . . . that is, your Queen, has enemies, very
powerful enemies. Do you know that a very
personal token of her esteem that I had the
honor of wearing at a ball a week or so ago—
two of a set of a dozen diamond studs—well,
these two (the rest remain in her own hands), as
I have just confirmed, are missing. And all the
evidence points to one conclusion: they have
been stolen, stolen by one in whom I had placed
great trust—the Comtesse de Winter, lately returned from a soujourn in your country. I see
now that she must be one of the Cardinal's
spies—that is, your Cardinal Richelieu's."

"I was aware of his power and have learned of
his spies, but here in England . . . ."

"Yes, the Cardinal is a very powerful man indeed." The Duke went on for some minutes more. In the course of his explanation, he described this Comtesse de Winter at greater length. Suddenly D'Artagnan started.

"You say this Comtesse—she goes by the name, in my country, of the English word 'Milady'?"

"Yes—why, do you know her?"

"I begin to think I have met her." D'Artagnan thought back to his unfortunate stop in Meung on the way to Paris, the mysterious gentleman there and the even more mysterious lady in the coach, headed, as it now seemed clear, for the Channel and England.

"My Lord Duke!" said D'Artagnan warmly, "You may be sure that if ever I should have the fortune to encounter this lady again, I will do all in my power to see that she is brought to justice. Not, you understand, for your sake, and not for mine— for the Queen!"

The Duke rose, D'Artagnan following him to his feet. Extending his hand to D'Artagnan, the Duke said, "Again, well spoken! I see we are in complete sympathy! For the Queen!"

He explained further to D'Artagnan what his accommodations would be for the next two days, and what D'Artagnan would then be expected to take back with him to France.

4

Mme. Bonacieux Is Kidnapped

TWO MORNINGS later, D'Artagnan found himself and Planchet leaving a small fishing boat in a secret cove near Boulogne-sur-Mer on the French side of the Channel. The Duke's power had helped him overcome every obstacle imposed by the Cardinal. He approached with some trepidation a tiny inn down an obscure path, his hand by his sword, expecting to be set upon by a gang in service of the Cardinal. He approached the innkeeper—indeed, the gloomy-looking bearded man was practically the only soul in the remote spot, save for a few grooms in the stable and some other servants—and, assured he was facing the right man, according to the Duke's description, softly mouthed the word—in English, though he was on French soil—"Forward." The man immediately showed he understood, nodded, welcomed him, and showed him to a pair of fine horses well stocked with provisions for a long journey, including a pair of pistols. The man carefully gave directions to the next resting place where again the password was to be spoken and the horses changed, and wished him a good journey.

As D'Artagnan and Planchet galloped down a network of little-used roads, getting ever close to Paris, the wind whistling in their faces, D'Artagnan from time to time fingered a little pouch at his side and felt satisfied. This was the means for saving the honor of the Queen, and it seemed that his goal would be reached. (Although he was ignorant of all of the Duke's arrangements he correctly suspected that the pouch held a pair of clever counterfeit replacements for the stolen diamond studs.) As he went along he also had time to wonder about his companions—whether Athos, Porthos and Aramis really had survived the encounter with that party of rogues in the Cardinal's service posing as road laborers. In this way they galloped on, raising clouds of dust behind them and drawing rivers of sweat from the flanks of their overworked horses. By dark they were on the outskirts of Paris, having covered an astounding sixty leagues in twelve hours. Determined to waste no time, D'Artagnan sent Planchet ahead of him and proceeded directly to the secret gate in the Louvre that he had been shown before. Knowing just the right words and the persons to see, he was admitted by the back stairs to a small private chamber. There he sat and waited impatiently for some time.

At length a young girl, well dressed but evidently still a servant, though of a higher order,

explained to him that he must wait in semidark-
ness for a while, and then he would see what to
do. After she had departed, D'Artagnan noticed
that there was a curtain on one side of the room,
behind which evidently was a door through which
some light seeped. He fancied the light getting
stronger. Then, to his surprise, a female arm and
hand, of exquisite loveliness, emerged from behind the curtain. At once he knew what to do. He
grasped a little packet in which was enclosed
the results of his mission, and placed it in the
hand, which disappeared behind the curtain. He
was about to withdraw, but the hand returned
and beckoned him to remain. In another few
moments the hand again appeared holding a
small object. Had an outside observer been
present, that observer would have witnessed at
that moment a scene that might have occurred in
a church. In the half-light, D'Artagnan knelt by
the hand, in which could be seen something that
glittered with an extraordinary radiance like an
exquisite gem, which in fact it was. D'Artagnan,
after receiving the gem, planted a light, respectful
kiss on the marble-like fingers as they withdrew.

It was the crowning moment of his life thus
far. D'Artagnan well knew the Queen herself had
personally bestowed upon him this precious re-
ward. Evidently he had returned with exactly
what was necessary to assure her happiness.

At last he stood up straight and examined the
gift; it was a ring, which he at once reverently

D'Artagnan, after receiving the gem, planted a light,
respectful kiss on the marble-like fingers.

placed on his finger. He paused for another moment in uncertainty, but just then the young girl from before reentered and quietly conducted him out of the Louvre by a back way.

As D'Artagnan strode home through the dark streets of Paris, he reflected on what had occurred. But he also thought back to his friends the Musketeers and began to think of how he might determine what had been their collective fate. He also wondered about the fair Mme. Bonacieux. Would he soon be seeing her as well? Would she demonstrate her gratitude for his having aided her royal mistress? As he mused upon all this, D'Artagnan began to be increasingly aware of his great weariness. He had endured much, and he longed for rest, which he would soon have at last.

Yet rest was not to come so easily. Expecting to arrive at his lodgings, tumble into his bed, and sleep for twenty-four hours—at least that is how severe his need for rest seemed to him—he forced himself to stride in his dust-caked boots ever faster through the dark streets of Paris.

Scarcely had he arrived at his doorstep when Planchet emerged.

"Monsieur, I thought you would never return," said he in a loud, agitated whisper. "First, I must inform you that all three Musketeers are alive—"

"Really? That is wonderful!" exclaimed D'Artagnan, his heart at once lightened by this good news.

"—Monsieur Athos has arranged to visit you this evening. There is much to be told."

"I am sure. But, tell me, Planchet, how is it that you will not let me into my apartment? Why all this down here? Could it not wait a few seconds?"

"You have, I am afraid, a visitor!"

"At this hour?"

"He did not come far—he had only to walk up the stairs."

"Bonacieux? What does he want from me at this time? His rent has been paid!"

"I thought I would prepare you, Monsieur, but now perhaps it is best to let the man himself explain."

D'Artagnan followed his servant up the stairs.

At the top of the stairs D'Artagnan encountered a short, balding, slightly plump man of about fifty, bowing and trembling at the same time. This man, though D'Artagnan rarely saw him, he recognized as his landlord, the merchant Jacques-Michel Bonacieux.

"Monsieur, Monsieur, forgive this intrusion, but they have done it again! I am beside myself! What to do? What to do?"

"Done what?" said D'Artagnan impatiently. "Speak!"

"My wife! They have taken her away again! It happened only this evening, before your servant here arrived. Don't think I am not grateful to you for having saved her the last time! Yes! But if you can help me find my wife again, you will not have to worry about the rent here for a long time."

There was no help for it. D'Artagnan had to listen to this man's pitiful wailing. But as we know, he had his own motives for finding Mme. Bonacieux, and he was, in his outwardly calm way, himself disturbed about this new turn of events. He urged the merchant, who continued to complain, to enter his apartment and sit down. When the latter had quieted down somewhat, D'Artagnan said, somewhat testily:

"All this groaning and wailing is of no use. Do you have any idea who was responsible for this abduction?"

"It is all political! My wife, as you know, is a servant of her Majesty the Queen, and I am sure that this is the work of the Cardinal. Alas! that I ever let her get involved . . . . But then again, my wife is a very headstrong woman. She never listens to anything I say! I knew this would happen! I knew it!"

"Come, come! We are getting nowhere. Can you describe any of the men who are responsible for this? Cease your whining and think!"

There was silence for a moment as the merchant was obviously struggling to contain himself. Then he said: "Well, I think I did notice that there was one who seemed in command. He had black hair, a dark complexion. A man of very lofty carriage, you see . . . . Ah, yes! I remember now! The man had a scar on his temple . . . ."

At this, D'Artagnan started. The description fitted that of the mysterious man of Meung, his nemesis! At first it was only a suspicion, but then the matter seemed confirmed when Bonacieux went on:

"In fact, Monsieur, I think I have seen the man before. Yes, I believe he is the same man my wife once pointed out to me as a man to beware of, a man who does the evil bidding of the Cardinal!"

"Well!" said D'Artagnan. "Now we are getting somewhere. I believe I know the man myself. You may rest assured, M. Bonacieux," said he, rising, "that I will not be satisfied myself until I have found this man and restored your wife to safety. But for now, you must leave me and be patient. There is much to be done, but it is too late to act immediately." At last the landlord rose and retreated down the stairs.

D'Artagnan sat for a while. Thoroughly exhausted after all his recent traveling, he did not remain awake much longer, but was resolved to ask the advice of Athos when he saw him later and to get to work finding the unfortunate Mme. Bonacieux as soon as he could. It would not, however, be simple. He knew he was swimming in dangerous waters.

5

Athos's Terrible Story

THE NEXT morning, or, rather, afternoon, when Planchet had finally roused him, provided him with nourishment and fitted him to return to his ordinary existence, D'Artagnan called upon M. d'Essart to resume his duty with the King's Guards. Before he arrived there, he was several times tempted to change his course and immediately run off to find Mme. Bonacieux—only he had not the slightest idea where to begin the search. He must ask Athos's advice in this matter.

Among his old companions in the Guards, as well as the Musketeers he met in the street, he fended off all inquiries about where he had been. But attention was distracted from such a minor matter as his unexplained leave of absence. Practically all talk that day was of the grand ball that the King was to give that very evening for the Queen. A grander affair had never been seen in Paris, it was said, and preparations had long been underway near and in the Louvre to provide the spectacles, the decorations, the music and the food for all the nobility of Paris.

Most of D'Artagnan's compatriots in the Guards had extra duty that night; it was only M. d'Essart's understanding indulgence of one of his favorite men that permitted D'Artagnan to be excused, as he had only just returned from his exhausting mission abroad.

That evening D'Artagnan was pleased to receive as his guest Athos, as planned, only there was a surprise visitor as well: Porthos. The latter had a bandage around his shoulder and limped in, helped by a cane. After they had been seated awhile and had expressed their mutual delight that they were still capable of meeting like this, they began to enlighten each other about their adventures after the time they were separated in the battle with the false road workers.

"You would not believe how bad the food can be at a country inn!" bellowed Porthos, who, wounded in the encounter on the road, had to spend time at one such place.

"Porthos complains of the food at country inns," said Athos. "However that may be, you may be certain that the wine is truly abominable. Aramis and I had to spend the night at one on our return to Paris after we dispatched those devils on the road, and there is never anything to drink at those places worth bothering about."

At this hint from a man who, as D'Artagnan knew, loved his wine, D'Artagnan had Planchet go downstairs and procure some bottles of a very fine vintage from Bonacieux. Athos, tasting the first glass of many, observed, "This is very good wine. How is it that your landlord is so quick to provide it? I thought you were on bad terms with him ever since you had so much difficulty paying the rent on time."

"I do not think that Bonacieux, tight-fisted as he is, will stint us this pleasure. I am sure he will be kind to me now, for reasons that I will explain shortly.

"But where is our friend Aramis? I am glad that he has remained with us, but have you not heard from him?"

"Aramis has aspirations to sainthood!" exclaimed Porthos.

"Or at least to holiness of some kind," continued Athos. "He was wounded, but has recovered. I do not think he has recovered from the wound to his spirit, however. After he killed two of those treacherous workers—"

"And a quick job it was, let me tell you! Aramis always was a good swordsman!" added Porthos.

"—he began to repent all the bloodshed, or so he says, and he has resumed his studies under some abbé in order that he may take holy orders himself."

"This will not last," said Porthos. "Listen to me! One word from his secret mistress—whoever the devil she is—and the four of us will be together again, let me tell you!"

"Be that as it may, at the moment he has, in his words, renounced worldly affairs. We scarcely see him."

Soon Porthos took his leave, remarking on his departure, "You know, gentlemen, we had best be looking after ourselves. For soon we may have the chance for great distinction in battle. I hear word at M. de Tréville's that M. the Cardinal remains dissatisfied with the rebelliousness of the Huguenots at La Rochelle. I think it likely he will persuade His Majesty to gather his forces and put down the troublemakers once and for all."

"Then let us indeed prepare ourselves," said D'Artagnan. "I only hope that Aramis will once again feel the spirit of a warrior and join us on the field of glory."

When Porthos had left, Athos opened another bottle of wine, and he and D'Artagnan sat down again.

"Do you know," said Athos, who even before he had begun to drink had been more talkative than was his custom, "that the Cardinal has suffered a blow?"

"What do you mean?" asked D'Artagnan, though he sensed what was coming.

"As you know, this was the day of the ball for the Queen. No doubt at this moment the nobles of the kingdom are enjoying a late supper. Well," continued Athos, pouring another glass, "I had the opportunity to look in during the grand ballet in which the King and Queen performed. Her Majesty looked stunning, by the way, and His Majesty looked absolutely his finest. Well, just before the ballet began, something passed between the two and the Cardinal. It seemed to be about some jewelry the Queen was wearing. Nobody could hear what was said but the face of the Cardinal bore signs of mischievous glee. The King at first seemed very angry, but something happened in which he counted some diamonds the Queen was wearing. He then seemed confused and turned to his Eminence the Cardinal. Then the Cardinal seemed angry and the Queen appeared to radiate joy. Finally the King and Queen appeared reconciled, while the Cardinal wore a face of gloom afterwards."

All the while Athos was relating this, D'Artagnan showed a gleam in his eye.

"Just as I thought, my friend," said Athos, looking directly at D'Artagnan. "You know more than I do, and you were not there. This incident would not, by any chance, have anything to do with your recent mission to England?"

"I think, Athos," replied D'Artagnan, "that you know the answer to that question. Although it is true that there are details of this affair with which I am unacquainted—and would not be at liberty to divulge even to you if I *did* know them—I think we may all rest assured that the trouble we took in that matter, all the risk of our lives on the road to Calais, has not been in vain. Behold!"

D'Artagnan raised his hand, displaying the ring that he had received only the day before.

"My God!" exclaimed Athos. "You did not get

that magnificent gem from anyone of a station lower than—"

"Exactly, Athos. The Queen. Of course this must be known to none but us four. Although this ring was given to me alone, the donor could not have known of the invaluable assistance I received in helping her. Naturally, you may be sure that if ever you or any of us is in need of money, I will sell this ring for what it will bring and—well, what is mine is yours."

"I am grateful for the thought, D'Artagnan, but if I were you I would not part with that gem for anything. It must be worth a King's—or rather a Queen's ransom!" Suddenly, Athos raised his glass and almost shouted, "A toast! A toast to her Majesty the Queen!"

The suddenness of this vociferation made D'Artagnan aware of two things: first, that Athos, having already dispatched the contents of almost two full bottles of wine, was beginning to show their effects; and, secondly, that although he had imbibed much less than his friend, he was beginning to feel slightly intoxicated himself. Then he felt sad.

"Something is troubling you, my friend?" asked Athos.

"I am afraid, Athos, that I cannot hide my concern. In fact I had wished to speak to you about this. Mme. Bonacieux, the wife of my landlord, has been kidnapped once again."

"And why should you be so concerned about

the wife of your landlord, D'Artagnan? What is she to you?" When D'Artagnan offered no reply to this and his face showed signs of darkening in anger, Athos continued, "I knew it! Beware, my friend. Danger lies ahead. He is old compared to her, she appears to favor you . . . . I know, but, as I say, beware!"

"I am afraid that this is love, Athos, and there is no helping it."

"And I suppose you believe that she returns your love? That she would willingly be your mistress? You child! Why, there is not a man who has not believed, as you do, that his mistress loved him, and there lives not a man who has not been deceived by his mistress."

"Except you, Athos, who never had one."

"That's true," said Athos, after a moment's silence, "That's true! I never had one! Let us drink!"

"But then, philosopher that you are," said D'Artagnan, "instruct me, support me. I stand in need of being taught and consoled."

"Ah! You wish to be consoled, do you? Taught, yes; consoled, I think not. I will tell you a tale, D'Artagnan, a tale that will make your blood curdle. But first, drink!"

As D'Artagnan hesitatingly raised his glass, he stared at Athos and wished that he had not ordered the wine, that he were someplace else, anything but this. For the lateness of the hour, the amount that Athos had drunk and something that evidently was weighing on Athos's mind connected with the story he was about to relate combined to lend a devilish cast to Athos's countenance. Athos was at a period of intoxication in which most ordinary drinkers begin to doze off. In a sense he *was* asleep, and yet wide awake at the same time. In what followed he spoke as if describing in vivid, horrible detail the contents of a nightmare that was at that moment passing through his feverish brain.

"This is a story, D'Artagnan, that happened to a good friend of mine, a count of the highest order. Not to me, you understand . . . to a friend of mine."

D'Artagnan hesitated to interrupt and Athos continued.

"This man was of the best of families. Unfortunately, he was also a man of honor. Why 'unfortunately,' you shall see. Well, at the age of twenty-five he fell in love with a girl of sixteen living in a cottage on his land. This girl was as beautiful as fancy can paint and had the mind of a poet. No one knew where she came from but since her one known relative—her brother with whom she shared the cottage—was a priest, and since it was rumored that she was of good family, her character seemed unimpeachable.

"Now, you understand, as so high-ranking a nobleman, my friend was also magistrate of his district as well as this girl's landlord. In effect, he was the law, and had he been unscrupulous he might easily have taken advantage of this nearly solitary girl with only her brother to defend her.

"But, no, he was an honorable man." An almost demonic undertone could be heard in Athos's voice as he softly repeated these words. "He married her." D'Artagnan sat transfixed, with a growing sense of horror, not knowing exactly what was coming but knowing it would be bad. Athos poured himself another glass of wine and downed it almost in one gulp.

"Well," continued Athos, "Not long afterwards, the newly married couple were out hunting. The young bride had an accident and fell from her horse. My friend, alarmed that she could hardly breathe, cut her restrictive clothing free at the neck. When a strip of cloth fell below her shoulder, what he beheld was the most horrifying sight he had ever seen. What had been concealed by the darkness of the marital bedroom was now clearly visible in broad daylight: the brand of the *fleur-de-lis!*"

Athos paused and looked into D'Artagnan's eyes. D'Artagnan just stared straight ahead, mesmerized. As he uttered not a word, Athos went on.

"The *fleur-de-lis*, as you know, is the brand of the Catholic Chruch for having committed one of the most horrible sins: stealing the sacred vessels from a church. It was immediately obvious that I—that is, my friend—had been deceived by a pair of the worst criminals in France. Well, at this

revelation, he lost control over his calmer nature
and immediately became judge, jury and executioner: in a fit of outrage, he tore part of her
clothing from her, twisted it into a rope, tied it
around her neck and hanged her from the nearest
tree."

"But Athos," said D'Artagnan finally, in a
scarcely audible voice. "That was murder!"

"No less. But if ever murder was justified—"
Athos paused to down another glass of wine.
"Her scoundrel of a 'brother,' who no doubt was
really her lover and accomplice and plotted with
her to secure her a position in the highest society,
soon vanished. But it may be hoped that by now
he too has been discovered and brought to
justice."

"Then—then, the girl at least is really dead?"

"It would appear so. Although I—my friend—
didn't have the heart to witness her last gasp, it
doesn't seem very likely that she would have
survived a hanging, does it?"

"My God, my God!" murmured D'Artagnan,
genuinely horrified.

"Well, this incident—hearing about this incident—has cured me of all beautiful, poetical and
loving women. God grant that you will take this
to heart and forget all about 'love'! Come! Have
another glass of wine."

6

A Conversation with the Cardinal

THE NEXT morning, D'Artagnan's head was spinning like a top. He knew not how the morning came, or how Athos had left; indeed, he scarcely remembered where he was, so affected was he by what he had heard the night before.

To steady himself, he forced himself to focus on one purpose: the impending battle at La Rochelle, for which he spent the next couple of days preparing. Of one thing he had no doubt: that he was honor-bound to serve his King, who, when he was not distracted by his favorite pastime of hunting, was exhibiting surprising enthusiasm for the battle. Of the part in all this played by the Cardinal, who no doubt had his own far-reaching schemes, D'Artagnan tried to think as little as possible.

At last the chilly morning dawned when D'Artagnan joined his troop of the King's Guards who, in a noble procession, began to make their way out to La Rochelle, where the stubborn Huguenots awaited the siege of their walled city. The noblest part of the procession, of course, was that in which the three Musketeers took their places in advance of the Guards, where D'Artagnan could not see them.

Just as Porthos had predicted, Aramis was among them, no doubt because he had indeed received the aforementioned word from his mysterious mistress. The Musketeers had all recovered from their recently acquired wounds and thought of the ordeal that lay ahead of them and the honors they might acquire.

As daylight broke on the troubled and tumultuous soil of France, D'Artagnan's heart was lightened when he saw before him the glittering arms and waving plumes of column upon column of His Majesty's soldiers. Over several days, with several stops at encampments and, for the officers, inns along the way, this mass of warriors gradually encroached upon La Rochelle.

Absorbed in his thoughts as he was leaving Paris, D'Artagnan had failed to notice three figures on horseback at the side of the road, one a lady, the other two men of obviously far lower station. Had D'Artagnan then looked to the side as he was moving along the crowded boulevard, he might have seen that the lady bore a striking resemblance to the woman he had briefly seen on a fateful occasion and with whose life his had become fatefully entwined: the woman called "Milady." Even then he could not have heard the whispers of the three, but, as the woman discerned D'Artagnan in the procession and indicated him to the two men beside her, and as the two nodded with a grim look, D'Artagnan might have been certain that their looks meant no good. In fact, as he had known when he risked his life for the Queen, he was indeed swimming in dangerous waters.

As he was quite unaware, however, of what was being planned for him, D'Artagnan's mood now actually lightened. At times he became quite confident that he would distinguish himself on the battlefield, eventually be reunited with the Musketeers, and even rescue Mme. Bonacieux.

At one point during some deployment of troops, D'Artagnan spotted attire and plumes that looked familiar to him.

"Aramis!"

The noble warrior on horseback turned at this exclamation. "So, D'Artagnan, it is you. I trust we shall meet on the glorious field of battle," said Aramis, for indeed it was he.

"Aramis, how glad I am to see you here, for another reason as well." D'Artagnan's mind had never ceased to dwell on the whereabouts of Mme. Bonacieux, in whom, despite Athos's cautionary tale, D'Artagnan had never once lost faith. At this fortunate meeting, D'Artagnan explained to his friend, who, it appeared, had secret connections in very high circles, the mystery of the abduction of Mme. Bonacieux.

"Alas, my friend," said the pious Musketeer, "I cannot work miracles. However, should God spare our lives a few weeks longer, I may be able to discover something that would be of help to you."

"You would earn my eternal gratitude," said D'Artagnan.

At this heartfelt utterance, before a word more could be spoken, the flowing river of soldiers parted in two and the noble friends had once again each to flow with his own stream.

At La Rochelle, the encampments were abuzz with a mixture of news and rumors. The Huguenots had been surrounded, but, though few in number, they were resisting fiercely. More of the King's and the Cardinal's troops kept pouring in, but the Rochellais maintained their resistance.

Through all this, D'Artagnan kept busy instructing his own troops and receiving commands from his superior officers. Thus far, all that had happened was generally expected. But then, one evening, as D'Artagnan was striding down an isolated road, the unexpected occurred. He saw three shadowy figures on horseback ahead of him.

"Who goes there?" came a shout from this group.

"Nay," returned D'Artagnan, who abruptly stopped, "it is for me to inquire of you, 'Who goes there?'"

The middle figure emerged from the shadows. Dressed regally, this was obviously no ordinary guardsman. Then he spoke:

"I perceive," said he, "that either you are a fool or you are unaware of the presence you are in. But I now see who you are, and I know, M. D'Artagnan, that you are no fool."

D'Artagnan stood in perplexity as to who this could be. Then moonlight glinted off a large cross on the man's chest, and suddenly, though he had never met the man, D'Artagnan knew whose presence he was in: that of the Cardinal himself!

Somewhat afraid—who wouldn't have been in such a circumstance?—D'Artagnan nonetheless mustered up his usual courage. His mind racing, he knew that his behavior in the next few minutes could affect his entire life. He removed his hat and made a low bow.

"Your Eminence," he said, "I did not recognize you in the dark. As you know, however, guarding this area is my responsibility."

The Cardinal did not answer immediately. When he did, his voice suggested a combination of nobility, shrewdness, nervousness and, as would be no surprise to his intimates, illness. Like the King, the Cardinal was perpetually wracked by a number of painful ailments.

"No doubt, M. D'Artagnan, no doubt. Indeed, I depend on your valor to guarantee my safe conduct through dangerous territory. Before we proceed, however, a word with you." He signaled his men to retire some distance and to D'Artagnan to approach him.

"What is it I can do for you, Monseigneur?"

"It is not, M. D'Artagnan, what you can do for me, but what you can do for yourself. I have just said that you are not a fool. I stand by that judgment. Nevertheless, it needs some qualification. You are, as one might say, somewhat impetuous and idealistic."

D'Artagnan was conscious of the intense scrutiny of the Cardinal, for no one had a more searching eye than the Duc de Richelieu. But he only nodded his head slightly and allowed the Cardinal to continue.

"That, at any rate," said the Cardinal, a trace of anger entering his voice, "is the only way I can explain your behavior when you meddle in affairs that do not concern you."

D'Artagnan restrained himself and still said nothing. He could not help reflecting, however, that what was said about the Cardinal's network of spies must in fact have a good deal of truth to it.

"Nevertheless, M. D'Artagnan," —now his voice softened— "you are evidently no ordinary young man from the provinces. Indeed, I admire your courage and your loyalty. Therefore, I am willing to make you an offer, which, from the nature of the circumstances, I strongly suggest you take: the commission of an ensign in my own private troop of Guards. I should be very pleased to have the protection of so capable and courageous a soldier."

D'Artagnan was hereby placed in a very uncomfortable situation. The Cardinal of course made this offer not so much to enable D'Artagnan to keep guard over him but so that he could watch over D'Artagnan. Nevertheless, to refuse the Cardinal's offer might be taken as an insult. He thought for a moment.

"I am indeed flattered and honored, Monseigneur. Nevertheless, as you yourself have said, I am loyal. I am already in His Majesty's Guards. All of my friends are in His Majesty's Guards or Musketeers. There is not—I say this since your Eminence appears to allow me to speak freely— the best of good will between the forces of the King and the Cardinal, and I should be ill received in one place and ill regarded in the other if I accept. I must therefore respectfully decline to accept your offer."

"I fully understand your decision, M. D'Artagnan. I will not press the matter. Nevertheless I will make an observation. You are young. Now, perhaps you shine in all your glory and you attribute it to your actions alone. Someday, you will come to realize the importance in life of your friends— and enemies. If you had accepted my offer, you would, I dare say, have had the benefit of the guidance of one older and wiser than you. As things stand now, I cannot answer for your safety." With these cautionary, indeed threatening words, the Cardinal motioned to his men, turned

D'Artagnan was placed in a very uncomfortable situation.

and rode off. Naturally, D'Artagnan was somewhat disturbed by this vague threat, yet he was
satisfied that he had held his ground and, indeed, remained loyal to his King and his prin-
ciples.

7

An Important Discovery

THE FOLLOWING day, D'Artagnan, though he
certainly had not forgotten his encounter
with the man who was at that moment perhaps
the most powerful in France, had enough to
occupy his attention. Already, as he was drilling
his troops, he noticed that he was being observed
by M. d'Essart. But not only M. d'Essart—behind
him stood Monsieur himself. Monsieur—that is,
the younger brother of the King—was overseeing
his brother's forces at this location and now
sought urgently a cadre of some of the finest
men for a mission of particular importance. It
seems that some of the most obstinate of the
Rochellais may have remained to defend a forti-
fied position that was originally thought to have
been evacuated. The bastion in which they were
believed to remain was in a dangerous position,
and anyone approaching it might receive a bullet
in his head for his curiosity.

Monsieur walked behind M. d'Essart, up and
down among the troops. As they stopped next to
D'Artagnan's men, Monsieur was heard to say to

M. d'Essart, "I want for this mission three or four volunteers, led by a man who can be depended upon."

"As to the man to be depended upon, you see him before you now, Monsieur," responded M. d'Essart, "and as to the three or four volunteers, Monsieur has but to make his intentions known, and the men will not be wanting."

The moment had come for D'Artagnan to distinguish himself, and he did not hesitate for an instant.

"Four courageous men who will risk being killed with me!" said D'Artagnan, raising his sword.

Two of his comrades of the Guards immediately sprang forward. Somewhat to his surprise, two other soldiers of a lower rank then appeared from he knew not where and eagerly volunteered to risk their lives with his. After some moments, a few other soldiers offered to add themselves to the company, but D'Artagnan, thinking he could best oversee the mission with the original four volunteers, thanked the others and declared to M. d'Essart that he was ready to depart on command.

As the five set out down the line of a trench, D'Artagnan tried to suppress an uneasy feeling. He was worried less about the danger of the objective than about something strange in the two unknown volunteers—exactly what, he could not tell. Perhaps it was his having to trust his life to men he knew nothing about, whereas his companions from the Guards he had drilled and mounted guard with for months.

The five marched on in silence. At a turning of a corner in the trench, the bastion loomed ahead. Nothing indicated whether it was indeed occupied. Then D'Artagnan heard a whisper at his side. It was one of his companions directing his attention, not to the bastion, but to the rear: the two soldiers had disappeared! Aha! thought D'Artagnan, so their cowardly hearts have betrayed them after all. Their hasty volunteering was merely a show of bravado. Well, perhaps undertaking the mission with only two trusted companions would ultimately be best. Not losing a moment, the stouthearted three continued to advance.

Suddenly the giant stone fortress was enveloped in smoke, loud crackling rang out, and a dozen bullets whistled around the heads of the three men. That was all they needed to know; the bastion was guarded after all. To remain longer in this spot would have been imprudence, not courage. The three turned in unison and commenced a rapid retreat.

Just as they had turned the angle of the trench that would shield them from further attack, one of the Guardsmen fell. He had been hit by a bullet after all! The other continued around the corner of the trench, safe and sound, headed for the camp. D'Artagnan, however, did not have the heart to abandon his comrade. He stopped abruptly and stooped to raise him and assist him in regaining the lines. At that moment, however, two more shots were fired, one almost grazing his head. D'Artagnan's first impulse was to duck. As he paused to think what to do next, however, a strange feeling came over him. Those bullets had not come from the bastion but rather from the rear! He glanced over the trench behind him and all at once knew what was wrong with those two soldiers who had turned back and whose heads he now discerned looking out from an abandoned pit. They were hired assassins whose sole purpose was to kill him!

Two more shots rang out. His thoughts moving as quickly as the bullets, D'Artagnan dropped, falling upon the body of his comrade as if dead.

In a few moments the assassins approached D'Artagnan to be sure he was in fact dead; after all, he might only be wounded and live to denounce their crime. Fortunately, deceived by D'Artagnan's trick, they had neglected to reload their guns.

When they were within a few paces, D'Artagnan, who in falling had taken care not to let go of his sword, sprang up. The assassins, too, thought quickly. If they were to flee back to their own camp—which was also D'Artagnan's—without having killed their man, they should be accused by him; therefore, it was to the enemy that they decided to run. One of them, flailing at D'Artagnan with the barrel of his musket, by this means managed to throw D'Artagnan off balance and make his escape. The other bandit was not so lucky. D'Artagnan managed to wound him in the thigh and he fell.

On the other hand, the luck of the first bandit ran out very quickly. The Rochellais, ignorant of his intentions, fired upon him, and he fell with a bullet lodged in his shoulder.

Meanwhile, D'Artagnan had the point of his sword at the throat of the second man.

"Do not kill me!" cried the bandit. "Have mercy! I will tell all."

"Wretch!" cried D'Artagnan. "Speak quickly! Who employed you to assassinate me?"

"A woman whom I do not know, but who is called 'Milady.' "

Stunned at this revelation, D'Artagnan almost dropped his sword. His situation was becoming all too clear to him.

"But," he continued, "if you do not know this woman, how do you know her name?"

"My comrade knows her, and called her so. It was with him she agreed; he even has in his pocket a letter from her. I have heard him say that she attaches great importance to you."

"But how did you become concerned in this villainous affair?"

"He proposed that I undertake it with him, and I agreed."

"Simply proposed it? Come, how much money were you offered for this enterprise?"

"Well, a hundred livres."

"A hundred livres!" D'Artagnan almost laughed out loud. "Well! She thinks I am worth something. That would be temptation indeed for a pair of wretches like you; I am almost inclined to pardon you."

At these words, something like a flicker of hope flashed across the countenance of the bandit, and he appeared about to rise. Immediately the point of D'Artagnan's sword was again at his throat.

"Not so fast! Perhaps I shall pardon you. But only on one condition."

"What is that?" asked the soldier, uneasy at perceiving that all was not over.

"That you go and fetch me the letter your comrade has in his pocket."

"But," cried the desperate bandit, "that is only another way of killing me. How can I go and fetch that letter under the fire of the bastion?"

"All right," cried D'Artagnan. "I will show you the difference between a man of courage and such a coward as you. Wait here. I will go myself."

This maneuver required considerable agility, as well as planning, to avoid the most exposed areas. As D'Artagnan darted in zigzag fashion along the trench, bullets again came flying. But once again, he had an inspiration. When he reached the dying man, he immediately hoisted him onto his shoulders, making of the man's body a shield. As they returned, the crackle of a bullet, the feeling of a jolt, and the final cry of agony from the man wrapped around him made D'Artagnan certain that this scoundrel, who would have killed him, had now, in perishing himself, saved his life!

Once around the bend of the trench, D'Artagnan could wait no longer. He lowered the man, now a lifeless corpse, searched him and came up with a wallet in which was the following note:

Since you have lost sight of that woman, and she is now safely in the convent, which you should never have allowed her to reach, try, at least, not to miss the man. If you do, you know that my hand stretches far, and that you shall pay very dearly for the hundred livres you have from me.

There was no signature. Nevertheless the origin of this villainous writing was very plain. As he made his way back to the wounded survivor of the two would-be assassins, he mused on its implications. This Milady understandably bore him ill will for having foiled her scheme to aid the Cardinal against the Queen. But the length to which she would go in her vengeance was obviously extreme. She was no opponent to trifle with, and his life continued to be in real danger.

On the other hand, there was good news in this note that lightened his spirits considerably: "that woman" whom the note referred to was almost certainly Mme. Bonacieux! She was now

The origin of this villainous writing was very plain.

"safely in the convent." Surely Aramis, with his connections in the church, would now better be able to assist him in rescuing her.

When D'Artagnan reached the man who was waiting for him he made up his mind to say nothing about the attempted assassination. More than his dead companion who had arranged the matter, this man seemed misguided by temptation rather than truly evil.

When they arrived at the camp, they were at first greeted with astonishment, since the first man to escape the Rochellais' bullets had honestly thought that his companions had all been killed. Then D'Artagnan was acclaimed a hero, and for a day the whole army talked of nothing but this expedition. Monsieur himself personally paid his compliments to D'Artagnan, who once again basked in glory. Through it all, however, his thoughts kept turning to how he could rescue Mme. Bonacieux.

8

A Perilous Breakfast

SEVERAL DAYS passed. The flurry and scurry
of war kept D'Artagnan busy, and the flying
bullets and flailing swords of the Rochellais kept
him from brooding about the threat to his life
from a less predictable and more sinister quarter.
Several positions of the Rochellais had been
overcome, and the number of their dead continued to increase. Though a few strongholds
continued to be occupied, signifying that the war
was not over, a lull came.

One evening at this time Planchet brought a
note. It was from Athos and it read:

> Must see you soon to relate glorious exploits
> of war. Tomorrow morning you will find us at
> the Parpaillot.
>
> ATHOS

This was a curious sort of note coming from
Athos, who was not one to boast of his accom-
plishments. Something else was certainly on
Athos's mind, something that he dared not put in

a letter. But this was opportune. D'Artagnan himself had for a long while been bursting with things to discuss with his friends.

Therefore, early the next morning, D'Artagnan, who was fortunately now able to get away from his troops for a short time as a result of the lull in the fighting, headed to the Parpaillot, an inn near the camp that officers of all sorts were known to frequent.

Little did he imagine the result of his meeting with the Musketeers, who were indeed all there. Before he knew what was happening, Athos had them agree to a bet with a rival group of four officers that they could spend an hour at the recently taken but still dangerous Bastion St. Gervais.

"All right," said Athos at the inn. "We four shall shortly proceed to the bastion and consume our breakfast there, remaining for a full hour. If we emerge a minute before then, we buy the four of you breakfast tomorrow. If we stay, provided that we survive, it is for you to provide us with the breakfast. Agreed?"

"Agreed!" said the leader of the rival officers. He and Athos then shook hands.

Athos silently motioned to his lackey Grimaud, who was standing in a corner frequented by the servants. In his usual quiet manner, Athos let Grimaud know what he was to do, and thus it was that in fifteen minutes the four were to be seen, armed to the teeth, walking down the path to the bastion St. Gervais. Grimaud followed with a large basket containing breakfast.

Porthos and Aramis seemed a bit uneasy. As for D'Artagnan, his head was spinning. When they were out of earshot of the curious group of soldiers who watched them depart, Aramis leaned over to Athos and said, "Do you know what you are doing? If it is really as the man says, even we are foolish to go up against a hundred Rochellais!"

"My dear Aramis, do you think I would risk our lives for nothing? All will go well, I promise you." Athos paused for a moment. They were approaching the bastion where, for now at least, all was quiet. "Now, can you think of a better way for the four of us to discuss our private affairs without risk of being overheard?"

No one could contradict this. There seemed, indeed, no other way to accomplish their purpose.

Their feet crunched over loose pebbles as they filed into the half-ruined fortress, and an odor of gunpowder lingered in the air.

"Aha! So, my friend, you knew!" said Aramis with a smile when they were inside. He referred not so much to the sight—ghastly to be sure—of more than a dozen dead men, but rather to the fact that these unfortunate soldiers were heavily armed. What with the muskets and powder and bullets, which Grimaud began collecting as soon as he had spread out the breakfast upon a stone bench, they had ammunition enough to fend off a hundred Rochellais.

After they had been eating their breakfast for a few minutes, D'Artagnan looked at Athos and said, "Well, I don't suppose you really sent that note to provide an opportunity to brag of your exploits. However, what I have been unable to tell you until now I think you will find most interesting. There has been an attempt on my life—"

"—No doubt that accursed woman had something to do with it," interjected Athos.

"What! How do you—"

"Hush!" said Aramis. There had been a noise. Now there could be heard in the distance the tramping of feet on gravel. All laid down their breakfast, picked up their muskets, and scrambled to the front wall. Sure enough, a troop of half a dozen soldiers was advancing upon the bastion, expecting to find it empty. All of a sudden one of them looked up and let out a cry, and they all opened fire upon the fort. But the Musketeers and D'Artagnan, as well as the faithful Grimaud, were ready. After a few minutes of crossfire, three of the soldiers lay dead and the others had beaten a hasty retreat.

"Gentlemen," said Athos, "our breakfast is unfortunately cold by now. Nevertheless, let us make the best of it.

"Yes," Athos continued when they were seated, "D'Artagnan, my friend, all our lives are in danger so long as this demon of a woman is alive—Yes, D'Artagnan, I know more than you think." As he said this, a grim look came over his face and he swallowed a glass of wine. Immediately this brought D'Artagnan back to that horrible night and Athos's nightmarish tale.

"You no doubt remember a tale I told you about a 'friend' of mine. Well, as you must have realized, that friend was myself. And that woman, whom I thought was safely in her grave, is alive."

D'Artagnan's glance immediately darted from one to the other of the Musketeers.

"Yes, all of us now know the truth. If I can trust any of God's creatures in this world they are with me now. And by this time I think you will agree that Grimaud has proved his loyalty. Now, I think you will also agree that it is our duty to search out and bring this fiend in human shape to justice.

"It will not be an easy task. Somehow, she has become involved in the Cardinal's schemes. Moreover, she is slippery as an eel. I thought that she could not leave this area without my learning of it, yet she has vanished as suddenly as she has appeared. I first suspected her presence in these parts several weeks ago, when she was evidently up to no good."

"As I should know," interjected D'Artagnan.

"Yes, but then she vanished, only to return as mysteriously a few days ago."

"But," said D'Artagnan once again, "can you

be sure that we are talking about the same woman? Not that this woman called 'Milady' is not—"

"I can absolutely attest to her identity," replied Athos. "For I have seen her. You see," he continued, glancing Heavenward, "there is some justice left in this world. I was placed in a position to overhear a conversation between her and the Cardinal at the inn a few nights ago. Then I surprised her when she was alone before she could escape."

He paused a moment, a grim look on his face.

"I would have strangled her right there but— where would be the proof of my justification in doing so? This is not so easy a matter. Meanwhile, however, I had a good look at her and she at me. From her reaction, I know she recognized me. And, moreover, I did force from her, at the point of my sword, this."

He drew from a hidden pocket a piece of paper—wrinkled, but obviously of fine quality and with the seal of nobility. On it D'Artagnan read:

> It is by my order and for the good of the State that the bearer of this has done what he has done.
>
> RICHELIEU

D'Artagnan looked up. "This is incredible! Could it be . . . ?"

"Yes, it is a *carte blanche* from the Cardinal

himself. I do not know what story she concocted to obtain such a document from him. I do know that with it she would be able to claim the lives of almost anyone. No local magistrate or officer of the law would dare go against the written word of the Cardinal."

"In fact," said Aramis, "it is an absolution according to rule."

"The first thing to do," said D'Artagnan, who saw in Athos's hands his sentence of death, "is to tear that paper to pieces."

"On the contrary," said Athos, "it must be preserved carefully. I would not give up this paper if covered with gold. You see, this is a two-edged sword that now may be used to our purpose. Meanwhile, I must build a more certain case against this woman. She has, at all events, vanished again from these precincts, in part probably because I know too much of her past. Yet the time must come soon when we bring her to justice, or else there is no doubt that she will act first. As you see, she has already made an attempt on your life. If she meanwhile contrives a plot against any of the rest of us . . . ."

Athos broke off, turning to Aramis.

"There is something else for our young friend here, is there not?"

Now it was Aramis's turn to bring forth a piece of paper. This was a letter, and far neater in appearance than what Athos had just displayed. The writing was a woman's, and D'Artagnan read as follows:

My Dear Cousin,

I think I shall make up my mind to set out for Béthune, where my sister has placed our little servant in the convent of the Carmelites. This poor child is quite resigned, as she knows she cannot live elsewhere without the salvation of her soul being in danger . . . .

And more of the same. It was signed by one "Marie Michon." D'Artagnan looked up at Aramis. A ray of hope shone within his heart. "Then this is about . . . ?" Aramis simply smiled slightly and nodded as he hid the paper.

The message to D'Artagnan was clear: Mme. Bonacieux, who was obviously referred to by a sort of code, had been located by Aramis's religious associates, and was now living under some kind of protection at the above-mentioned convent.

"Gentlemen, I would be honored," said D'Artagnan, "if, when you possibly can leave your duties for a time, you would assist me. For many reasons I believe that Milady may cause grave harm to be done to my beloved Constance." This was Mme. Bonacieux's first name. D'Artagnan recalled vividly the words he had read in the letter he had retrieved from the dead man who had made an attempt on his life.

"Yes, D'Artagnan," said Athos quietly, "we must act as quickly as we can. Once this fiend of a woman discovers Mme. Bonacieux's hiding place, if she has not already, one may not give two sous for the young woman's existence. Shortly I shall try to communicate with some friends of mine near the convent who may help us in bringing the consequences of the acts of a she-devil onto her own head. —What is it, Grimaud? Yes, you may speak!" His servant, whom he had trained to be silent in all but the most exceptional circumstances, was motioning vigorously from his position near the wall of the bastion that faced the town.

"Monsieur, it appears that an enormous army is advancing upon us. Let us get out of here while we may!"

All of the Musketeers but Athos jumped to their feet. Athos rose more slowly, saying, "Fear not, my friends. I have an idea." He glanced at his watch. "Fortunately we have been here over an hour." He pointed to the corpses of Rochellais strewn about the floor of the bastion. "I believe we have here a fine troop of soldiers, do we not?" He hoisted one of the bodies over his shoulder and propped it in an upright position overlooking the outlook in the wall.

"By George, that's the way!" shouted Porthos, as he and the others scrambled to arrange their massive bluff.

"Now let us take our belongings and depart without undue haste," said Athos, as a shot rang out at the lifeless figure now taken for a living soldier. "This puppet show will give us the time to depart this place like men!" Methodically, after having fired a few shots of their own out of the fortress, the four filed out of the rear entrance, Grimaud following with the remains of their breakfast.

As they neared the lines of their own side, Athos said quietly to his companions, "By now the Rochellais have discovered our ruse and retaken the bastion. It is a desperate move that cannot ultimately gain them much. But, as for ourselves, I think we are now in a position to look forward to a fine breakfast tomorrow morning! Gentlemen, in about two or three days I hope to have some news and some plans worked out. Meanwhile . . . ."

"Athos, Aramis, Porthos, how can I thank you?" exclaimed D'Artagnan. "For now I shall be silent and patient, with hope in my heart."

The four then rejoined their compatriots, a certain four of whom, in a state of amazement that the Musketeers and D'Artagnan had returned unscathed, were almost uncaring that they had lost their wager.

9

A Devilish Adversary

D'ARTAGNAN WAS now perforce separated from the Musketeers for a while, but the opportunity to rejoin his friends soon came in an unexpected way. One morning a summons came from M. d'Essart, who with a strange look in his eye gave D'Artagnan leave to see M. de Tréville. Though M. de Tréville was always like a benevolent uncle to him, D'Artagnan could not imagine the reason for this summons. He was careful to be on his best behavior as he entered the inn where M. de Tréville was headquartered, as this was also the wartime residence of the King.

D'Artagnan was asked to step into an inner chamber that was more lavishly decorated than anything he had been used to. Before he knew what he was about, he realized that seated before him on a cushioned chair was the King himself. Somewhat abashed, he started to withdraw, but M. de Tréville, who was standing next to the King, motioned him to step forward.

D'Artagnan made a low bow. Although Louis

XIII was still a relatively young man, he had a somewhat drawn look upon his face. As ever, this sign of frequent illness was mingled with impatience and boredom.

"Yes, step forward, young man. Tréville," he continued, turning his head to one side, "I suppose we must do what we must do. I am heartily sick of hearing nothing but tales of this D'Artagnan's acts of bravery. Now that the Cardinal has mentioned him as well, I suppose that we must do something to put an end to all the chatter."

The Cardinal! Could it be that a man whom D'Artagnan had come to regard as his enemy had spoken favorably of him to the King?

"Young man, you will henceforth report to M. de Tréville here, with whom I believe you are already well acquainted."

"Your Majesty, how can I ever express my gratitude—"

"Yes, yes, enough of this. Tréville, you will go with him now and make the necessary arrangements. Yes, go now. Ah, I am exceedingly sick of this place. Soon, soon I think we depart for Paris . . . ."

D'Artagnan's ears were ringing as Tréville led him out of the royal presence. It was almost too good to be true. Scarcely fully able to comprehend what was happening, D'Artagnan had suddenly been made a member of that elite group that had long been the embodiment of his highest ideals: the King's Musketeers.

Tréville had already spoken to M. d'Essart about D'Artagnan's departure. Later that day D'Artagnan bade farewell to his comrades of the Guards, wound up his affairs there, and transferred his belongings to the very inn at which his bosom companions Athos, Porthos and Aramis were quartered!

The Three Musketeers had now become the Four Musketeers!

His elation soon subsided, however, for a dangerous situation remained. Milady was still at large, and Mme. Bonacieux was still awaiting rescue. While this was so, D'Artagnan could not entirely be at ease.

Nevertheless, now that he was a Musketeer, it seemed to him that his goals, shared by his sympathizing companions, would be easier to realize. This was true; however, another occurrence that was out of their control—along with the actions of the perennially cooperative M. de Tréville—made these tasks much easier. The King, who was ever restless and easily bored, even by the noble call to war, decided to return to Paris, planning also to indulge in his favorite sport of falconry on the way. His personal guard of Musketeers was thus called away from La Rochelle before the Rochellais had been quite defeated. Since the band in its entirety was now superfluous, as even His Majesty had to admit, M. de Tréville managed to obtain permission to

The Three Musketeers had now become the Four Musketeers!

grant a portion of them leave. Naturally, the
favored four were the first to be granted this
leave. A pretext was easily found.

As the four rode, with their trusty servants,
toward the town of Béthune, some forty leagues
north of Paris, they had something new to talk
about. The Duke of Buckingham had been assas-
sinated!

"But why," asked D'Artagnan of Athos with a
feeling of dread in his heart, "do you believe that
Milady had anything to do with *this?*"

"That woman is a pure incarnation of evil. But,
more than that, she had every reason to bear him
ill will for having thwarted her scheme to dis-
credit the Queen."

"Or the Cardinal's scheme."

"Yes, most certainly, but you may be sure that
she entered into such a devilish plan as eagerly
as if it had been of her own devising. And
remember something else. Supposing that she
was involved in this, she is now free to cook up
more deviltry."

"And therefore, as you continue to insist, I
should not attempt the rescue of Mme. Bonacieux
alone."

"You are the very soul of courage and loyalty,"
said Aramis, "but I agree with our friend Athos.
We have to do here with a woman whose pro-
pensity to evil is almost more than human. Your
success in achieving your goal is, more than is
ordinarily the case, in the hands of a Higher

Power. But it is just as much our duty to assist you as best we can."

These observations struck a chill into D'Artagnan's heart. D'Artagnan was afraid of no mortal; but an adversary who was a devil in human form . . . .

About four o'clock in the afternoon, a few hours before the four expected to reach Béthune, another incident occurred in the courtyard of an inn, where they were preparing for the final stage of their journey. Another gentleman emerged from another part of the same inn and mounted his horse. D'Artagnan caught a flashing glance of this man's countenance and froze: it was his nemesis, the man from Meung, the blackguard who had more recently been involved in the abduction of Mme. Bonacieux. It was for but an instant that D'Artagnan's blood froze in his veins. In an instant more, his sword was drawn and he was inches from the horse on which the man had mounted.

"You scoundrel! Draw your sword and fight like a man!" shouted D'Artagnan.

The man, startled by this outcry, turned in his saddle and, when he perceived D'Artagnan, did, in fact, draw his sword to ward off the impending attack. But at almost the same moment he dug his spurs into the flanks of his horse, seized his hat, which had almost flown off his head, and charged out of the courtyard.

D'Artagnan ran back to mount his own horse,

to the astonishment of his companions. But then he stopped, for in his better judgment he understood the futility of his efforts. The man had gotten a head start on a fresh horse, and, moreover, was headed in a different direction. To pursue him now would mean the indefinite postponement of his present mission.

As D'Artagnan and the other Musketeers stood in a circle discussing this new development, Planchet approached them.

"Excuse me, Monsieur, for interrupting," said he, "but I think this will interest you," handing over a folded piece of paper. "It fell out of the hat of the departing gentleman."

D'Artagnan read what was on the paper and then passed it around to his friends. Written on the paper was only a single word: "Armentières."

"What can this mean?" D'Artagnan was perplexed.

"Armentières," said Aramis, "is the name of a town, not very far from Béthune."

"The devil if anyone knows what these puzzles mean," said Porthos, "but hadn't we best be on our way? Béthune is still a ride of a few hours from this place."

"My friends," said Athos, retrieving the paper, "I think that it has been our great fortune to have this paper. I cannot say for sure, but I do believe that, if this man is he whom D'Artagnan thinks he is, as I have no doubt, this paper may soon prove to be worth more than its weight in gold.

"But, yes, for now we must continue on our mission. It is all the more urgent if such a man as this has been seen so close to our destination. As things are, we can only pray that we are not too late."

As the sun was setting, they had arrived at last in Béthune, and the four were now riding down the winding path from the gate of the Carmelite convent to the main building. The Mother Superior proved to be a well-bred, cultivated woman and seemed glad to receive visitors in that lonely spot.

"Well," said she, "this most pleasant young lady whom you wish to see has been the cause of our receiving more visitors here than we are accustomed to. Why, just yesterday a most distinguished guest arrived, a Comtesse de Winter, who professed a great interest in the young lady. They may be together as we speak."

At this revelation all four Musketeers jumped slightly and exchanged meaningful looks. D'Artagnan immediately inquired as to where they might visit Mme. Bonacieux and, once directed to the correct path, ran rather than walked to the building, his companions lagging behind.

D'Artagnan called out Mme. Bonacieux's name. Receiving no response, he opened the door, which had been left slightly ajar.

"M. D'Artagnan, is that you?" came a faint woman's voice from the other end of the room.

She was still there! Indeed, there she sat in an

armchair. And no one else was in the room. D'Artagnan was not too late!

In a wave of passion, he ran to her and partly lifted her from the chair.

"You need fear no more! You are under my protection now! But—what is the matter?"

Something was in fact wrong. Mme. Bonacieux wore a look of ghastly paleness and seemed hardly able to move or speak.

She stared into his eyes and murmured faintly, "D'Artagnan! D'Artagnan! Do you know? I have loved you all along!"

Could this truly be? D'Artagnan impulsively drew her to him and planted a lingering kiss on her precious lips.

But suddenly he felt her body grow limp in his arms.

"She . . . she's dead!" he murmured, as a sense of horror froze his blood in his veins. Kneeling beside the lifeless figure, he lifted his hands in prayer. "Oh, just Heavens! Can this be?"

"I'm afraid it can," came a familiar voice from behind him. He turned his head and saw that his friends had arrived. Athos, who had spoken, stood by a table examining a glass that had been there. "Poison!"

"Poison! But why?"

"I have said we are dealing not with a creature of God but rather of the devil." A grim look passed over his face as he murmured through clenched teeth, "There will nevertheless be an end to this. There must be an end." He put his arms around the still trembling D'Artagnan. "My friend, I must ask you to have patience. Bear up like a man. We will see that Mme. Bonacieux receives a decent burial." D'Artagnan began to shake uncontrollably. "Then, though it is little comfort to you now, I think finally we may see to it that justice is done."

"With the help of the Lord," said Aramis, crossing himself.

There was a guest house where the four remained for a few days. Meanwhile, Athos was strangely absent for a good part of the time.

"Our friend," said Porthos quietly to Aramis, "knows more about this than he lets on."

"Is that not always the way with Athos?" replied Aramis.

10
Milady

ALL IN ALL, the next few days were like none other that D'Artagnan ever spent. He passed hours transfixed before the coffin of his beloved Constance Bonacieux, racked by waves of weeping. Athos was frequently absent but when he returned from his mysterious outings he lost some of his typical reserve and was like a father or elder brother to D'Artagnan.

"Weep now, my boy. Have your fill of weeping," he said one time, secretly wishing he could experience such relief himself. "Soon it will be time to have your vengeance like a man."

It was indeed a strange time. After a while D'Artagnan noticed that not only was Athos absent, none of the four servants was to be seen either.

"Yes," said Porthos, "my Mousqueton is away as well. But it is necessary. Our friend Athos must have his little schemes, eh?"

Finally, having bid his last heart-wrenching good-bye to the spirit of his beloved, D'Artagnan followed the others, like an automaton, he knew not where. Athos had rejoined them and they set off. They spent a morning at an inn a few leagues from Béthune.

"If we may now be permitted to know, exactly where are we headed?" asked Porthos.

"Do you remember," said Athos, "it now seems ages ago, when the faithful Planchet discovered this paper" —he now held it before them— "with the one word 'Armentières'? Well, there is a God in Heaven, for it is by this paper that justice will be done."

"Is . . . she in Armentières, then?" asked D'Artagnan.

"Yes, and under close surveillance. She will not escape us now. But, as far as I can tell, she has no suspicion that she is watched. Remember that, although she knows very well who we are, she is not likely to recognize our servants."

With this remark, some of the clouds of mystery began to clear, and D'Artagnan thought he could begin to understand something of what was going on.

In a moment, however, D'Artagnan again felt himself surrounded by mystery. A man walked in the door, unfamiliar to D'Artagnan but obviously with the dress and behavior of a man of rank. Yet no one seemed to know him.

"Gentlemen," said he, with a slight English accent, "since I am obviously not known to any of you, I must inquire—does one of you go by the name of M. Athos?"

At this inquiry, Athos's face showed a sign of recognition. "Ah, yes, I was expecting you, my lord." "My lord"—so he was a nobleman!

"Allow me," continued Athos, "to introduce my fellow Musketeers, Porthos, Aramis and D'Artagnan. My friends, this is Lord de Winter, who at my behest has come here from England."

De Winter! D'Artagnan had reason to know that name: the Duke of Buckingham had remarked to him that that was the real name of the woman often called "Milady"! D'Artagnan thought that now he could comprehend a little more of the mystery. But the relationship of this man to Milady yet remained unclear.

Lord de Winter, for reasons still known only to Athos, became a member of the party that soon set out for Armentières.

D'Artagnan still felt a chill at his heart, but Athos, whom he thought of as an older brother, inspired confidence in him like no other man, and D'Artagnan followed him without hesitation.

Indeed, Athos himself had every reason to be emotionally distraught at the recent turn of events, given especially the recently revealed connection with his own past. Yet now were his noble qualities, his self-control, his gift of command over others and over every detail of a complicated operation, in evidence as never before.

Before arrival at their final destination, which was still known only to Athos, two stops had to be made. The first was yet another small inn on the outskirts of Armentières.

"What is it that we have to do here?" inquired Aramis.

"Wait," replied Athos, consulting his watch. And they did little but that for two or three hours more. Had D'Artagnan not still been in a state of shock, the suspense would have been unbearable. As it was, Porthos did nothing but pace back and forth the whole time.

Then, when darkness had fallen, the five rode to a deserted spot on the other side of town, where there stood a dilapidated cottage just off the road. Here Athos bid them wait a moment more, and shortly he returned from the cottage with yet another member of the party.

The newcomer was an elderly man with a long beard, wearing a black hood that partially concealed his face. He said not a word. Yet another mystery! The group—now six—rode on.

Ultimately they arrived at their final destination, an even lonelier cottage in the middle of a remote field. It seemed that the cottage, visible in the moonlight, was deserted. Then D'Artagnan thought he could see a flicker of light behind a curtain in a window.

Suddenly a figure emerged from the shadows and approached Athos. It was Bazin, Aramis's manservant!

"She is there," he said softly to Athos.

"Very good," replied Athos in a whisper. "And the back door?"

"Mousqueton is posted there. Grimaud and Planchet will now join us."

"Excellent. Gentlemen, let us go."

Athos knocked several times at the front door, but there was only silence in response.

"We shall have to break down the door, I'm afraid," said Athos.

This was not too difficult, as the little wooden door was old and the latch weak.

When they entered, a young woman with ruby-red lips and a pale face surrounded by black hair jumped up from a table on which stood a flickering candle. Her beauty sharply contrasted with the squalor of her surroundings.

"Who are you? What do you want from me?" she gasped.

D'Artagnan was astonished by what he saw and by the entire situation. Could it be that they were making a grave mistake? He was not even certain he recognized this woman as Milady.

"We want justice," proclaimed Athos in a stern voice. "And you know very well who we are. You also know the crimes for which you have to answer."

Though Milady was a consummate actress, alarm showed in the flickering of her eyes around the room. Still, an innocent woman surprised by a strange band of men would show alarm as well as a guilty one.

"It has been many years," continued Athos, "and perhaps you don't recognize me. But you know your brother-in-law, Lord de Winter, and—"

With a little gasp, she turned and attempted to bolt out of the back door, only to come face to face with Mousqueton. Grimaud and Planchet, who had entered behind the Musketeers, seized her arms. Soon she was again seated, Bazin pointing a loaded pistol at her head.

"If you have come for vengeance," she cried, "how can you be certain you are not mistaken? Your—"

"It is not vengeance we desire but justice. We have sufficient proof." He pointed to the mysterious man who had recently joined them. "This man has the ultimate proof of your identity. You may remember him as the Executioner of Lille."

Milady let out a stifled gasp but otherwise remained silent.

"Let us begin," continued Athos, "and have done with this hideous business. I shall start the proceedings.

"Charlotte Backson, *alias* Lady de Winter, *alias* Milady, you are hereby accused of the following crimes. First, you married me under false pretenses while living in sin with a man you falsely claimed was your brother and while you were in secret a branded criminal. D'Artagnan, you next."

D'Artagnan, transfixed by the horror of all this, nevertheless mustered his courage, stepped up and, drawing out the paper he had taken from his would-be assassins, said:

"And I accuse you, first, of having murdered Constance Bonacieux in cold blood. Second, I accuse you of having attempted to have me murdered, as this paper proves."

"Good," said Athos. "Now, Lord de Winter . . . ."

De Winter stepped forward, rage written across his face. "I accuse you, first, of having falsely married my brother, the late Lord de Winter, although you were already married, and, then, of having murdered him for his money. Second, I accuse you of having inspired a crazed fanatic to assassinate the Duke of Buckingham. This murderer, a man I had entrusted to keep watch over you, had been in my employ, and I shall regret that the rest of my life. Nevertheless the guilt remains on your shoulders. I believe you are next, sir." He looked at the strange man who had last joined them.

"Charlotte Backson," he began in a cracked voice, "or shall I still call you the Comtesse de Fère?" The Comtesse de Fère? Here at last was the missing link. Although Athos had revealed much of his past to his friends, implying that he was of high birth, he had never actually told them his real name. The Comte de Fère! That meant that he represented one of the noblest families in France. When the Musketeers began to realize the significance of this, they darted inquiring looks at him. D'Artagnan thought he perceived only a faint nod in response.

*"I accuse you, first, of having murdered Constance
Bonacieux in cold blood."*

Meanwhile, the former Executioner of Lille continued, "You may or may not remember me, although I think you do. For it was I who branded you in punishment for your sacrilegious act against the Church. And it was my brother who was the priest whom you seduced into living with you in sin. And then, when you thought he would turn against you for having murdered Lord de Winter, you poisoned him." He turned to Athos. "Is that all?"

"Yes. It is more than enough to justify what we are about to do." He looked at the servants. "Seize her and bring her outside."

This they did. At first she began to struggle like a trapped animal but soon saw that it was no use.

"Wait!" cried D'Artagnan, touched by her relative youth and, if truth be told, her beauty. "Can it not be that we are making a terrible mistake? Death is final. If given another chance she may repent . . . ."

Athos stepped between Milady and D'Artagnan, facing the latter, his hand on the hilt of his sword.

"D'Artagnan! You are to me like a brother. Yet were you my blood brother, my own son, I would sooner run this sword through you than let this fiend go unpunished." D'Artagnan knew that Athos was right, and said nothing more. In a softer tone, Athos then said, "Perhaps you will want to wait here with Porthos and Aramis. The rest of us will not be gone long."

Porthos put his arm around D'Artagnan and led him to a chair as the others marched out the door.

About five minutes later a muffled cry came from the distance.

In another few minutes Athos returned alone. "The others will attend to the disposal of the body. We may now depart."

Slowly, the other Musketeers rose and filed out of the door to retrieve their horses.

"Gentlemen," said Athos, "soon, I assure you, we will feel relief as we realize that the world is now rid of a demon. This has not been a pleasant task, but at last justice has been done. We may now return to Paris."

Of my story, little remains to be told. D'Artagnan had been afraid that when the execution of Milady became known to the Cardinal, he and his companions might end up in the Bastille for their audacity. Instead, the Cardinal was relieved to be rid of an accomplice whom even he had had difficulty keeping under control. The Musketeers were allowed to go their own way. D'Artagnan in fact soon was surprised to receive a commission as a lieutenant.

Alas, this was at first of little comfort, for he soon had to say farewell to his friends. Athos returned to his old life as the Comte de Fère, living on a distant estate. Porthos, on finding that the husband of his "duchess" had died, proved his loyalty by marrying the woman, and soon he departed the Musketeers to live on her inheritance. Aramis kept his faith with the Church and retired to a monastery. D'Artagnan eventually became captain of the Musketeers, an ever-courageous but older and wiser man.

Of the King, the Queen, the Cardinal and the nation of France—their fate is history.

THE END